www.hmhco.com

The illustrations in this book are linocuts and digital mixed media.
The text type was set in Rotis.

Library of Congress Cataloging-in-Publication Data
Names: Huang, Rebecca, author.
Title: Bobo & the new baby / by Rebecca Minhsuan Huang.
Other titles: Bobo and the new baby
Description: Boston ; New York : Houghton Mifflin Harcourt,
[2018] | Summary:
When his owners bring a baby home, Bobo the dog competes for attention.
Identifiers: LCCN 2016014697 | ISBN 9780544713581 (hardcover)
Subjects: | CYAC: Dogs—Fiction. | Babies—Fiction.
Classification: LCC PZ7.1.H75 Bo 2017 | DDC [E]—dc23
LC record available at https://lccn.loc.gov/2016014697

Manufactured in China
SCP 10 9 8 7 6 5 4 3 2 1
4500679145

Bobo
and the
New Baby

written and illustrated by

Rebecca Minhsuan Huang

This is Bobo.

Bobo likes his life.

He likes to snooze.
He snoozes
on the sofa.

He snoozes in
the bathtub.

He snoozes in
the laundry basket.

He likes to chase.
He chases birds. He chases butterflies.

He chases the mailman.

But what he likes
most in the world
is Mr. and Mrs. Lee.

Mr. and Mrs. Lee love Bobo too.
They take him everywhere.
They do everything together.

Until one day,
Mr. and Mrs. Lee
come home with . . .

a BABY!

Bobo
has never seen
a baby before.
He circles,
he barks,
he jumps.

"Stop, Bobo!
You will scare the baby,"
says Mr. Lee.

Bobo walks away.

Bobo wants attention, but . . .

Not now, Bobo!
Baby is eating.

Not now, Bobo!
Baby is changing.

Not now, Bobo!
Baby is sleeping.

Not now, Bobo!
Baby is crying.

Bobo watches and waits
        and waits
            and waits.

But then . . .

Buzz

Buzz

Buzz

There is a bee!

Bobo barks at the bee.
He chases it around the house.

He will not let it hurt the baby!

"Stop, Bobo!
No running in this room.
You'll hurt the baby,"
says Mr. Lee.

"Wait, darling.
There is a bee.
Bobo just wants to help,"
says Mrs. Lee.

"I'm so sorry, Bobo," says Mr. Lee.

"Bobo, do you want to say hello to the baby?" asks Mrs. Lee.

Bobo looks at the baby.
He looks sweet. He looks happy.
He looks just like the Lees.

And Bobo knows that he will love him.